Off We Go!

by Jane Yolen

Illustrated by Laurel Molk

Little, Brown and Company
Boston   New York   London

Tip-toe, tippity toe,
Over the leaves and down below,
Off to Grandma's house we go,
Sings Little Mouse.

Hip-hop, hippity hop,

Through the slime and over the slop,
Off to Grandma's, never stop,
Sings Little Frog.

Dig-deep, diggity deep,
Down where day is dark as sleep,
Off to Grandma's house I creep,
Sings Little Mole.

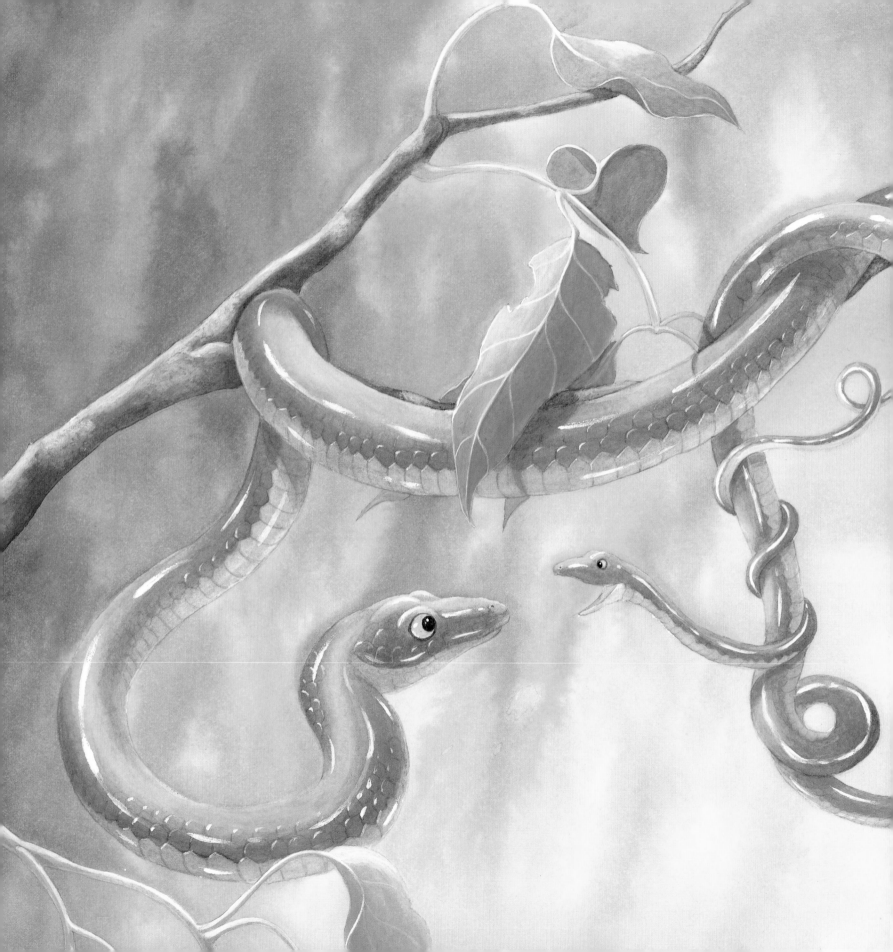

Slither-slee, slithery slee,
Down the branch and round the tree,
Off to Grandma's house goes me,
Sings Little Snake.

Scritch-scratch, scritchity scratch,
Directly from the egg I hatch,
Then off to Grandma's house I dash,
Sings Little Duck.

Creep-crawl, creepity crawl,
From the web and down the wall,
Off to Grandma's house free-fall,
Sings Little Spider.

Tip-toe, tippity toe

Tip-toe, tippity toe
Hip-hop, hippity hop

Tip-toe, tippity toe
Hip-hop, hippity hop
Dig-deep, diggity deep

Tip-toe, tippity toe
Hip-hop, hippity hop

Dig-deep, diggity deep
Slither-slee, slithery slee

Tip-toe, tippity toe
Hip-hop, hippity hop
Dig-deep, diggity deep

Slither-slee, slithery slee
Scritch-scratch, scritchity scratch

Tip-toe, tippity toe
Hip-hop, hippity hop
Dig-deep, diggity deep
Slither-slee, slithery slee

Scritch-scratch, scritchity scratch
Creep-crawl, creepity crawl

Wherever Grandma's house is found —
In hole, in tree, or underground,
In web, or bog, or in a nest —
Why, Grandma's house is *always* best.